TEDDY
and
The Flying Circus

Teddy gazed up at a sky of clear blue,
At a silver speck coming into view.
The speck began to hum like a bumblebee,
Then began to fall like a leaf from a tree.

The tiny speck grew larger and Teddy could see,
A glittering aeroplane with a bright red 'B'.
The plane flashed low just above the trees,
Causing branches to dance in the breeze.

Then it soared up high into the blue,
Trailing vapour as upwards it flew.
It dived and looped the loop, banked and spun,
Yellow wings glittering in the sun.

Then flying slowly
          The plane dived low,
"Golly," thought Teddy,
          "what a great show."
Beaming from the cockpit
          And after looking all around,
The pilot brought his gleaming
          Machine, safely to the ground.

The pilot stepped down from his cockpit
          and said, "Hello, you young bear,
my name is Captain Bogglesworth
          and I've just come from over there.
I lead a flying circus and I'm looking
          for a place without hills,
where we can put on a flying display
          and demonstrate all our skills."

"I'm pleased to meet you, sir,"
Saluted Teddy with a smile.
The captain said, "Call me Boggles,
my friends do all the while."
He was dressed in white flying leathers,
A bear of the air indeed.
His goggles, moustache and silken red scarf,
Declared a special breed.

Teddy was very excited and said,
"Do you think that this field will do?"
"It looks perfect to me," said Boggles,
"but I must fetch the rest
of the crew."

He climbed back into the cockpit.
And soon the engine spluttered
and roared,
With a smile and a wave
to Teddy,
He sped across the field
and soared.

Teddy rushed off to tell his friends,
     About the exciting events of the day.
He told them about Captain Boggles
     And his aerobatic flying display.
Jimbo said, "Wouldn't it be lovely
     If we could go up in a plane."
Teddy said, "I'm sure that we can,
     I'll ask when I see Boggles again."

The next morning the bears assembled,
                By the edge of the field,
They waited for signs of the aeroplanes,
                Their ears and eyes peeled.
Suddenly they heard the engines
                And the sky above them revealed,
Planes of all types and vintages
                As round and round they wheeled.

One by one they landed
      And taxied till they stopped,
Boggles waved to Teddy
      As to the ground he hopped.
He then introduced his pilots as:
      "A very daring bunch,"
Then invited Teddy and his friends
      To join them all for lunch!

Teddy was admiring Red
      Baron Bear's plane when
Boggles cried, ''Today!
      We must make our plans
for next weekend, to give
      a grand flying display.''
''A good idea!'' said Teddy.
      ''But I have something
important to say,
      can you teach me to fly
an aeroplane Boggles,
      by next Saturday?''
Boggles laughed and said,
      ''Why not?
It shouldn't take too long.
      I'll make a pilot of
you I'm sure,
      follow me and you
cannot go wrong!''

"Since there's no time
like the present,
let's go up for a
spin right now.
You can sit in front
of me,
and I will show you how."

Red Baron Bear cried, "Contact!"
And gave the propellor a swing.
Off they taxied across the
Field and Boggles began to sing!

Soon they were soaring
        High in the sky, climbing
With tremendous power.
        Teddy looked down at
The village church and
        Saw Vicar Bear in the tower!
Boggles said, ''Now I will
        teach you to fly, it's
as simple as can be,
        just keep paying attention,
listen carefully and follow me.''

Teddy followed his instructor with care
        And quickly began to learn,
By moving the controls to the left or right,
        The plane was made to turn.
Pushing forward the plane dived low
        And pulling back the plane climbed high.

Teddy was having a marvellous time
　　　　With Boggles in the sky.
Boggles said, ''Well done young Ted,
　　　　now I think we'll take her down.
You have earned your wings as I knew you would
　　　　and you'll soon be the talk of the Town.''

When the great day came
　　　　And the circus took to the air,
The Pilot bears performed
　　　　With intrepid skills so rare.
They flew daring aerobatics
　　　　For all the spectators to view,
And then with vapour trails
　　　　Streaming, etched patterns
Of red, white and blue.

Then Captain Bogglesworth announced,
    "Now is the grand finale!"
It was to be performed by Teddy,
    Jimbo, Belle and Bessy.

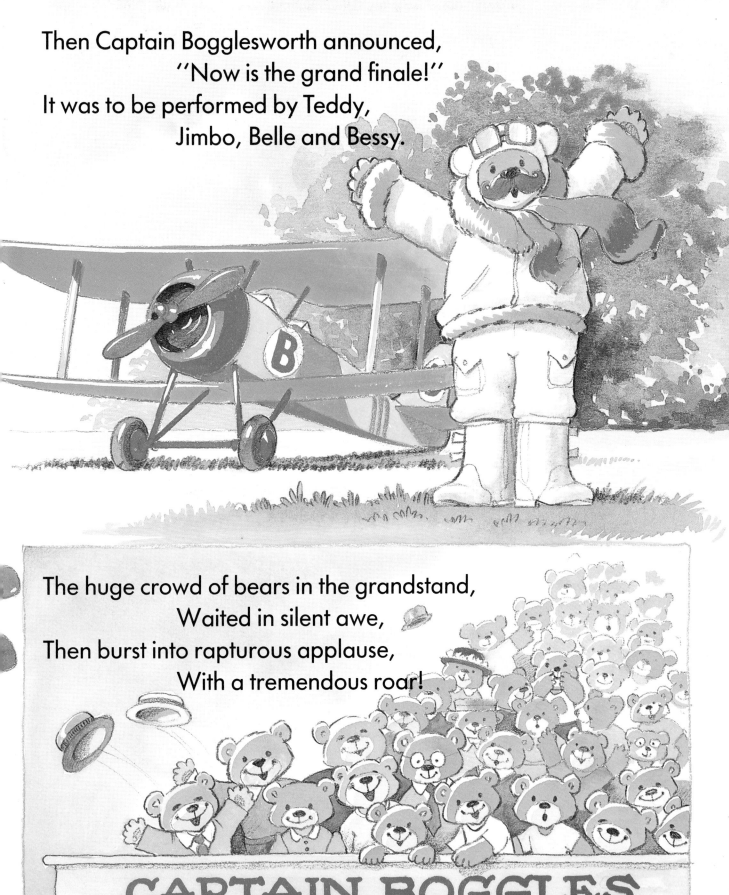

The huge crowd of bears in the grandstand,
    Waited in silent awe,
Then burst into rapturous applause,
    With a tremendous roar!

CAPTAIN BOGGLES
FLYING CIRCUS

Skimming over the trees
            And humming like a bee,
There flew a silver plane
            Marked with a big Red 'T'.
Teddy smiled and waved from the plane,
            Jimbo did as well,
And standing on the
            Wings were little Bessy
And Belle!

There were claps and cheers and hats in the air,
    For their magnificent feat,
And Boggles said, "Ladies and Gentlebears,
    that was certainly a treat.
We have had a lovely time,
    entertaining you one and all,
and tonight you must come,
    to our Flying Circus farewell ball."

The Teddy Bear ball was splendid
      And went off very well,
Teddy dancing with Bessy
      And Jimbo dancing with Belle.
The Lord Mayor Bear made a little speech,
      Recalling the daring scenes,
Of Boggles and his bears and their
      Magnificent flying machines.